HAPPY Winter

The Winter Spirit

By Gina Wood Joseph

Illustrations by Maxwell Heiderer

First Page Publications

The Winter Spirit is a storyteller and the Christmas myths, legends and historical information written in this book are meant to be his interpretation of the facts. As the wise old storyteller would say, "Better details can be found in texts, written by scholars who know how to explain–far more than I–what makes a reindeer fly!"

The author wishes to acknowledge
David Wood and Niky Hachigian
as collaborating editors.

Also Philip Van Hulle III
for contributing to the synopsis

Jacket and cover designed by Maxwell Heiderer and D.M. Joseph

Creative Photography By Helen
303 South Hamilton Street,
Saginaw, MI 48602
Helen M. Amy C.P.P.

Publisher's Cataloging-in-Publication

Joseph, Gina Wood.
    The winter spirit / by Gina Wood Joseph ;
illustrations by Maxwell Heiderer.
      p.cm.
      SUMMARY: Eleven-year-old Katie is starting to have
doubts about Santa Claus. Then she meets Hans who has a
snowy beard and knows an awful lot about Christmas. When
Katie finds Hans' lost book with children's letters to
Santa in it, she rediscovers the Christmas beliefs she
thought she had outgrown.
      ISBN 1-928623-42-5

    1. Santa Claus--Juvenile fiction. 2. Christmas--
Juvenile fiction. [1. Santa Claus–Fiction. 2.
Christmas–Fiction.] I. Heiderer, Maxwell. II. Title.

PZ7.J77924Win 2004   [Fic]

First Page Publications
12103 Merriman
Livonia, MI 48150
www.firstpagepublications.com

To Dave for his art and heart. You are the scan man.
To Dayna for her character and youthful insight.
To Justin for his constant smile and for giving me
all the time I needed. To the memory of my
parents who gave me Christmases to remember.

GLJ

To Gretchen for giving the coat life and for being the
first to believe. To Salvatore and Rosareo for giving me their
odds and ends. To Pamela for giving up her coat. The birch
tree for giving up a limb and to Heather and Ron for
believing in the gift giver.

MJH

To everyone who believes it's more fun to give than to receive!

Katie stared out the window at the falling snow. Like a cast of angels, the frosty white flakes fell gently from the sky. Her heart leapt as she watched the pageantry unfold. Up and down and all around the angels danced. Then off they flew, fueled by the whim of a northerly breeze. It was Christmas snow. Katie could tell by the way it flickered against the blue December sky.

itting on the bed next to Katie was a small box. She smiled at its covering of toys, trees, and elves crafted from construction paper, old Christmas cards, and glitter glue. She flipped the box upside down and emptied its contents. Ten letters tumbled onto the bed. Each one had a shiny sticker on the bottom right corner — some of them gold, some of them red. All of the letters were addressed to Katie from Mr. and Mrs. Claus on Reindeer Ranch Road.

Katie studied the stack with teary eyes. She loved believing in Santa Claus. It was the icing on her Christmas cake. "When I grow up, I want to be just like Santa," Katie said to her father, Erik. "I want to fly in a sleigh and shout, "Merry Christmas to all, and to all a good night!"

hat was Katie at 5.

Now that she's in middle school, things are different.
She has decided she wants to become a
veterinarian when she grows up and
she's having doubts
about Santa Claus.

There's no such person," said Katie's friend Joanie, while the two of them stood at the bus stop. "I can't believe your parents didn't tell you. Maybe it's because you have a younger brother and sister. Maybe they were afraid you would blab. My parents told me as soon as I was a teenager."

"You're not a teenager," Katie snapped. "You're 11, just like me."

Katie sat on her bed pondering Joanie's words. She wanted to believe her. After all, she was her best friend. And yet ...

No Santa? It made her heart ache.

"Besides, if there's no such person, who sent me these?" Katie said to herself, while looking at the letters stacked on her bed. She let out a big sigh, put the letters back in the box, and gave it a kick under her bed.

The snow angels were still dancing in the yard, only now the wind was howling after them. Katie pulled the curtains closed and cranked up the volume on her stereo. "Grandma got run over by a reindeer, walking home from our house Christmas Eveee," the song played on. Katie giggled at the thought of her grandma running down the road with a reindeer at her heels, then she grabbed for the big cardboard box that her father had brought down from the attic.
It was marked: Katie's Room.

Every year, she used its contents to decorate her bedroom Katie-style for Christmas. Her box of decorations included a small white church, a Santa Claus globe, and a nutcracker with a broken nose. These were the odd pieces her mother no longer used. Katie also had a Christmas doll dressed in red velvet, a large box of purple garland, clear twinkle lights, a small pine tree, and a dented cookie tin filled with miniature ornaments.

Dearest among the tin's tiny treasures were a hand-carved wooden polar bear and a Father Christmas figurine. Katie rubbed her fingers over the edges of the wooden bear. She had found it in her Christmas stocking the same year she visited the polar bear exhibit at the zoo. It was after that trip that Katie decided she wanted to become a veterinarian. She placed the bear on her tree.

ext was the figurine. She unwrapped the small porcelain piece and held it in the palm of her hand. It was one of the last gifts from her Grandpa Jack. He passed away a couple of years ago. Katie smiled, thinking about her beloved grandpa. He was a tall thin man, which was amazing considering his passion for cookies. Next to sweets, a good book and a hot cup of tea were among his favorite things.

She could see him now, sitting in the winged-back chair next to the fireplace, his long legs stretched out on the ottoman and his face buried in a Louis L'Amour western. Boy, how he loved to read. It's probably why he was such a great storyteller.

At Christmastime, Grandpa Jack's favorite tradition was to read to his grandchildren. Without fail, he would begin with his favorite story, "A Christmas Carol" by Charles Dickens.

"Ebineeezzzer!" Grandpa Jack would wail in his Scrooge voice, as he cracked the book's cover.

The children had favorites, too. Katie's little sister, Heather, adored the Nativity story. She liked to imagine how beautiful everything must have been on Jesus' birthday.

"Oh, Grandpa," Heather said. "Tell me about the angel and the Three Wise Men. Have you ever seen a camel? I wish I could see an angel. I wish I could have seen the big star in the sky."

"You can see the star," Grandpa Jack replied. "Just look to the east on Christmas Eve. You will see. One star shines brighter than the others."

Katie has a little brother. His name is Jack, too, but everyone calls him JJ. One Christmas after Grandpa Jack finished JJ's favorite story, "The Night Before Christmas" he pulled out three tiny packages. He handed one to Katie, one to JJ, and one to Heather.

"You know Shadow
Creek isn't the only stop
that Santa Claus makes on
his Christmas Eve journey.
He visits children in France,
Italy, and Australia, too.
Each country harbors its
own visions of Santa
Claus," he said. "He's
known as different things
to different people. I
bought each of you this
figurine because it reminds
me of the Santa Claus I knew as a
boy. My mother, your great-
grandmother, grew up in
England and called him
Father Christmas."

Katie placed Grandpa
Jack's Santa Claus on the
nightstand next to her bed.

Then she finished decorating her room. She put the tiny tree on her dresser and draped the garland and twinkle lights over her headboard. The final touches were the shiny silver snowflakes that she had fashioned out of aluminum foil during art class a few weeks before. These she hung from the ceiling using pieces of her dad's fishing line. "Awesome," Katie said, while lying on her back admiring the display.

That night, Katie had a wonderful dream. She dreamt that she and her Grandpa Jack dined with Father Christmas and his wife — who looked a whole lot like Katie's grandmother, Virginia.

She was sitting next to an elf. The table was covered with an amazing feast. She reached for a piece of the yule log cake...

"Hey, Katie Bear! How about coming for a ride?" Katie's dad called to her, while standing in the doorway of her room. He looked around, admiring his daughter's creative decor. "Come on Katie Bear, I have to drop a job off at the lodge and I thought you might want to come along. I'll treat you to lunch."

From beneath the cozy pink fleece comforter came a yawn, then a nose, then Katie. She sat up and threw her dad a great big smile. She loved how he called her Katie Bear. She asked him once why he called her that. He mumbled something about a teddy bear that she used to drag around the house, but Katie knew better. She was sure the real reason was that it had sounded neat to him the first time he had said it, and now he couldn't stop.

"Sure, but can I take my snowboard?" she asked, staring once again at the scene outside her room. A fresh blanket of snow had covered the hills around their home. Katie's dad owned a small printing company in the mountain resort where she and her family lived. They did all sorts of jobs, from travel brochures and ski passes to 'No Smoking' signs.

E rik drove around often to drop off work for his customers, and whenever it was some place fun, like the big ski lodge, Katie loved to come along.

On the way up the mountain, Katie and Erik passed a man hiking along the road. He used a long staff and looked like a shepherd tending his flock. He was wearing beige pants, a red coat and a white knitted hat. It had a red pompon. Katie marveled at the way he plowed along. Swish! Swish! Swish! He had white hair and a white beard. He looked old enough to be somebody's grandfather, yet he walked with the stride of a young man headed for the slopes.

"Who's that?" Katie said, while pointing to the snow-swisher.

"I believe his name is Hans Oberlin," her father said. "He's a history professor. When one of the professors broke his leg skiing, Mr. Oberlin offered to take over his classes at the college until he's able to return. He's staying at Eleanor's House out by the lake."

Katie studied the man. His smile. The beard. "He looks like ... like ..." Katie's voice trailed.

"Like Santa Claus?" Erik volunteered. "I know. Everyone is talking about him. Your mum said he stopped by the preschool while she was working and asked if he could read to the children. She told him they would enjoy that very much. He showed up the next day wearing some type of costume, carrying a wooden staff and a big book. The children were mesmerized by the tales he told of a man he called the 'Winter Spirit.'"

Katie watched the snow-swisher fade in the distance as her dad turned their truck into the next driveway.

The path was long, but once they were over the first hill, Katie could see the lodge, or her castle, as she liked to imagine it.

After a day on the mountain Katie could always be found in the lodge's great room. It's where the skiers and snowboarders gathered to warm their toes and boast about their latest feats. Sometimes, when the victors of the mountain looked to be the same age as Katie, she would join in the revelry.

ther times she would sit by the fire with a cup of hot chocolate, captivated by the mountainous tales.

Katie and her dad walked into the great room and took a deep breath. Ummm! Someone had just stoked the fire. Katie could smell the mixture of pine and cedar.

"OK, Katie Bear," her father said heading toward the offices, "I'll meet you in the dining room for lunch.

S tick to the paths and remember no yahooees! I don't want you to spend Christmas in a body cast."

The sun was still yawning as Katie jumped off the lift and headed to the top of her favorite run, The Beaute. It was a great time to be on the slopes. When the sun rises above the mountain's peak and its rays hit the frosty white flakes, everything glitters like silver and gold. As a little girl, Katie was told that the glitter was diamonds left by a traveling giant. He had mined them in Africa and was on his way home when he discovered that he had a hole in his saddlebags.

"What really happened," Katie's dad explained, "is that he tried to scoop them up, but the wind kept blowing snow over the top of them. Now, when the morning sun shines, melting the snow's top layer, you can see the diamonds left by the giant miner. People have tried to pan them, but by the time they get started, the sun is up and the diamonds are gone."

Katie stood at the top of the mountain in awe of what she saw. Then, the sun cleared the peak and the glitter was gone. It was Katie's cue. She pointed the nose of her snowboard toward the run. Then she smacked the top of her helmet, the usual sign for good luck, and headed down the slope.

"Yahoooeee!"
she hollered.

Katie carved three or four trails out of the snow before finally taking a break. At the bottom of the mountain there was a big stone fence. It marked the property line at Eleanor's House, a mid-century bed and breakfast owned by a woman named Eleanor Hows.

atie set her snowboard down and climbed the fence. She could tell that Eleanor wasn't home because the snowmobile that she used to travel to and from town was missing from its usual spot.

However, there was a glow in the windows and smoke coming out of the chimney. Perhaps the current tenant, the old snow-swisher, was in.

"What the heck," Katie said, jumping from the fence. "I'll just stop by for a visit. After all, it's the neighborly thing to do."

Katie tapped on the door's porthole window.
Nothing.
She tapped again. Still nothing.
She was about to leave when she heard a deep voice holler, "Come on in."

Katie entered the house and was met in the hall by a tall gentleman whose hair was rippled and as white as the snowy wave she rode down the mountain. He had one boot on and the other in his hand.

She couldn't help noticing the boots. They were a bright red and very soft — unlike anything she'd ever seen.

"Hello," he said, while hopping on one foot.

Katie let out a giggle.

"You'll have to excuse me," Hans said with a smile. "I'm planning to visit some children at the church and I figured they would want to see me in costume. So you see ... you sort of caught me in the middle of Santa morphing."

He was no ordinary Santa. Nowhere in sight were the red suit, shiny black boots, and wire-rim glasses of your typical mall-Santa. He was wearing a long green flannel shirt, ivory pants and hunter green socks.

"There," he said, tying up the laces on his boots. "Now, I'm all ready except for my coat."

Katie's eyes followed Hans as he turned and looked toward the door. Then she spotted it. Hung neatly on a hanger was an amazing coat.

Katie blinked. For a moment she'd thought that the coat was surrounded by a faint aura of light. Like a Christmas tree waiting to be plugged in, the coat looked like it was waiting to be worn. Whoever put it on was sure to light up the room. From where she stood Katie could see that the coat was a tapestry of patches, and it looked hand-stiched.

"Did you make that?" Katie asked.

Hans laughed. "Give me a piece of wood and a good carving knife and I can make just about anything. But give me a needle and a piece of thread and I'm sure to poke myself. No Katie. My dear sister, Gretchen, made this for me."

"It looks like something from England," Katie said.

"Actually, its design is German," said Hans, removing the coat from the hanger so Katie could inspect it further. It had white fur, gold colored thread and multicolored fabric patches. Hans told Katie that his mother had cried when she saw it because it was so beautiful and it reminded her of the great coats worn by the men in her homeland of Austria.

"Why don't you make yourself comfortable while I see if I can rustle up a couple mugs of hot chocolate," Hans said and headed for the kitchen. Katie was too excited to be comfortable and decided to follow him.

"My dad told me you were a history professor," Katie said. "Is that ummm ... your main job then?"

"Yes, I am a professor of history. But I'm also interested in many other things. Like flying, for example. I've been working on a new flying machine," Hans said, while putting the kettle to boil. Then he looked at Katie with an 'I've got a secret but I'll show it to you' kind of expression, and reached for a leather-bound book that was sitting on the table. The green book looked exhausted. As if it couldn't tell another story. Its pages were tattered and its leather covering was worn, like the sole of a hitchhiker's shoe.

Hans opened the old book and carefully pulled a page from its middle. It was a drawing. It looked like it could be an airplane or a sleigh.

"Tight" Katie said.

As Hans replaced the page, six or seven more fell to the floor.

"One of these days…" Hans sighed, "I'm going to find a way to have this book rebound."

Katie tried to see what was on the papers, but Hans was too quick. He picked them up and quickly tucked them into the back of the book.

T hen he slid the book to the other side of the table and hurried to the kettle which was now whistling Dixie. Hans poured them each a cup of cocoa and filled a plate with sugar cookies.

Cookies and cocoa in hand, the two retired into the living room.

"So Katie," Hans said, settling into a big armchair. "What do you like to do?"

"I love soccer and snowboarding," Katie blurted out excitedly. "Some day, I'd like to be an Olympic snowboarder. Today, my art teacher brought in a pottery wheel to show the class. I think I'd like to try that."

"Crafts are good. They cultivate the creative soul," Hans said.

He heaved himself out of the chair
and retrieved the wooden staff that Katie
had seen him walking with earlier that day.
Grinning, he held it out to Katie.
"I made this out of a birch branch,"

"Sweet," Katie replied.

"I use this as a guide when I go to
see my children," he said. "And I
look upon everyone as my children."

Katie studied the branch,
admiring the detail of each carving.
Tiny Christmas vignettes went from
the top all the way to the bottom of
the staff. Each one led to another
story about the life and times of
St. Nicholas.

"Tell me about the
tree at the top," Katie
asked Hans, who had
settled back into his armchair.

t's an evergreen tree," he said. "A symbol of life."

"We talked about that in school," Katie said. "My teacher told us that ancient people said it was special."

"That's right," Hans said. "People used to believe that the evergreen, because it didn't die in the winter, was sacred. That's why the evergreen is associated with the winter solstice."

"What's a solstice?" Katie asked.

"That was the holiday celebrated before Christianity, some 4,000 years ago," Hans replied. He was about to set the staff aside but seeing that Katie was so interested, he explained its carvings further.

"This little boat symbolizes Santa Claus as the patron saint of sailors," he said. "Legend has it that St. Nicholas magically appeared on several occasions to save the lives of sailors stranded by stormy seas."

Beneath the boat and the Menorah, a symbol of the Jewish Festival of Lights, there was a magnificent carving of the Nativity and the Star of David.

"Santa Claus was a very prayerful man," Hans said.

Also carved on the staff was an image of Mary and Joseph as travelers headed for Bethlehem. Below it was a reindeer. "What's with the reindeer?" Katie chuckled.

"Is that Rudolph?"

"The legend of Santa's reindeer comes from Nordic and Scandinavian mythology," he said. "In this part of the world, they believed that during the winter solstice Odin and Thor, the god of poetry and wisdom and the god of thunder, would fly through the air on reindeer and pass out gifts to the good people below."

Katie looked at her watch. It was only 11 a.m. She had an hour before she would have to meet her dad. She asked Hans if he would mind telling her one more legend.

"My pleasure," he said in the voice of a friendly bus driver.

Katie picked up the staff while he went into the kitchen for more cookies. She felt a thrill in her arms and imagined that she was Odin riding a reindeer.

"Yahooeee" Katie yelled, raising the staff.

Hans laughed, "Ho... ha... ha... ha!"

"How about this one?" Katie said pointing to a smiling face carved on the staff.

"Oh, that's one of my favorites," Hans said. "A long time ago, St. Nicholas had an assistant, a black man from North Africa by the name of Razi, which in Aramaic means 'my secret'. Legend has it that Razi was a Moor (someone of mixed Arab and Berber descent living in Africa) who converted to Christianity and became a disciple of St. Nicholas.

ince St. Nicholas was so busy, Razi helped him keep track of the list of who was naughty and who was nice. Many people also believe that it was Razi who helped St. Nicholas choose the right gift for each girl and boy."

"Really?" Katie said. "Wait until I tell my friend, Ayana. Her father is from Africa."

"You know, by now, most children I talk to would be asking me questions about the North Pole," Hans said. "You've been a great listener. I can tell that you must have someone in your family who tells stories too."

"My Grandpa Jack used to read me stories all the time," Katie said. "He said reading out loud was fun."

"I would have to agree with your grandfather," Hans said. "Every year, I make a point of visiting a few preschools, foster homes and public libraries. It is fun and it's my way of sharing the wealth. There are so many historical legends and stories that people have shared with me over the years. And you know Katie, there are many children who don't have people to tell them stories.

Hans stared at the fire, looking rather serious. Then his smile returned.

"I remember one year this young girl, around your age, came up to me and said, 'You're the real one, aren't you?'"

Then she said to me, 'What I want from you is to bring my family back together.' I told her that St. Nicholas believes in the power of prayer and that's what she would have to do if she wanted something really bad," Hans said.

"The following year when I returned to the youth home, she was gone. The director at the facility told me that her disappearance probably meant that the family had been reunited."

Katie looked Hans in the eyes. They twinkled like the diamonds left by the giant miner. Then, just as she was about to ask him if he really was the real one, a cuckoo clock on the wall started to chime.

Cuckoo!
Cuckoo!

It was noon. She had to go or
her dad would worry. Katie
finished her hot chocolate
and apologized to Hans for
keeping him so long. He
told her it was his pleasure.
Then he offered her a lift
in his van. Katie was
pleased to accept the ride.
She put on her boots and then
watched in amazement as
Hans settled into his coat,
pulled a matching hat trimmed
with white fur out of
one of the pockets and placed it
on his head.
    "There," he said with a wink.
"Now you can call me the
Winter Spirit.

atie was awestruck. It was like her Father Christmas figurine had come to life.

"Wow," she whispered. "You're really him." The Winter Spirit just smiled. "Most people want to believe in Santa Claus," he said. "Because believing makes the heart feel good." The last piece to the Santa Claus suit was a brown leather belt with jingle bells and a white pouch.

"I bet that's where he keeps the magic dust used to make the reindeer fly," Katie mused. Before leaving, the Winter Spirit picked up his big green book and carefully tucked it under his arm. Katie grabbed her snowboard and followed him out the door reluctantly. She wished her time with the Winter Spirit wasn't nearly over.

"I know you have a luncheon date at church now, but what about tomorrow? Do you think that maybe you can have dinner with us?" Katie asked.

"Thanks for the invitation, but I have to be home on Christmas Eve," he said.

Katie giggled and said, "I know. You've got toys to deliver."

The Winter Spirit smiled as he set his staff and big green book on the seat next to Katie. When they pulled up to the lodge Katie jumped out of the van, grabbed her snowboard, and thanked her new friend for a wonderful time.

aybe I'll see you before you leave," Katie said. "If I don't, have a great Christmas."

"You too Katie!" called out the Winter Spirit. Then he turned with a jerk and sped off in his red Chevrolet.

Katie was about to head up the path when she noticed a green object lying in the snow. She reached down and picked it up. It was the Winter Spirit's book! It must have fallen out of the van when Katie got out.

"Oh, dear," Katie said. "He'll be so worried."

Katie wiped the book off and took it inside the lodge. Then she called the church and told the Reverend to tell Hans not to worry. She had found his book. Then, barely suppressing a big grin, Katie headed to a chair situated in a corner of the great room, away from everyone. There, while waiting for her dad, and the Winter Spirit to call, she stole a peek at the book.

ithin the weathered binding she found personal notes, stories and fun facts such as time zones and wind speeds. There were Christmas legends, fables and tales. She even saw recipes for reindeer food and candy canes. What Katie found most interesting were the drawings and old letters. There were pencil sketches of sleighs, like those she had never seen before, and village buildings and toys. Katie studied one of the drawings closely. It looked like a toy crane. It had big wheels, a cab and a big scoop. There was a smaller picture at the bottom showing the same toy transformed into a fierce-looking T-Rex.

"Rrrr!" Katie whispered. "JJ would love a toy like this."

TOY AREA

REMOVABLE RIBS FOR BAG

LIGHT ON STEP.

*TALK TO THE AUTO GUYS IN DETROIT ABOUT LIGHTWEIGHT CUSTOM SEATS.
*MEET WITH AIRPLANE MANUFACTURER TO DISCUSS USING THE WIND TUNNEL.
*CHECK WITH NASA ON THE STATUS OF THE ROBOTIC TOY LIFTER.
*SEND A NOTE TO KEVIN: MOVE THE HOT CHOCOLATE DISPENSER TO PASSENGER SIDE.
*VISIT SKI MANUFACTURING PLANT TO TALK ABOUT NEW RUNNER MATERIALS.

TOY PLANS

CRANE TO PLANS

T-REX

In the back of the book was a pocket, like a secret compartment. It was stuffed with letters. Some of them were addressed to Santa Claus, others to the Winter Spirit. Katie had goosebumps. They looked very old. One of them had ink drops and elegant writing. Katie remembered when her English teacher had brought in a quill pen to her class one day to demonstrate the type of tools used by writers such as Shakespeare. Katie thought this letter looked an awful lot like the examples of quill-penned letters that her teacher had shown.

Dear Santa Claus,

I don't need a toy this year, as my grand ma-ma made me a doll for my birthday. But please bring my papa a new plough and ox. The bank took ours away and he needs it to finish the field.

Love, Patricia.

Another letter was sent by a little boy. This one was written with purple, red and green crayons.

Dear Santa,
Be carfool.

There was a picture of a stick boy, an address and an additional note:

P.S. Happy Christmas Santa, from Robert.

Katie was so excited about the book and the letters that she didn't notice her dad standing next to her.

"I take it that's the book Hans was referring to," her father said.

Katie's face turned red. She closed the book and explained what had happened.

"Daddy, you wouldn't believe it. I met Mr. Oberlin, I mean the Winter Spirit, while I was out snowboarding. I stopped at Eleanor's place and he told me all about the legends of Christmas and ... He made some hot chocolate ... Joanie said there's no such person but gee ... I mean his stories, this book ..."

"Slow down, Katie Bear," her father said, smiling at Katie's enthusiasm. "I know all about the book. Hans called from the church and told me you paid him a visit. He was happy to hear that you found it. He wants you to hang on to it for him. He said he'll pick it up next week."

Katie nodded as she cradled the fragile book in her arms. On the way home, she continued to tell her dad about her meeting with the Winter Spirit. She told him about the carved staff and all of the charities that the Winter Spirit visited during the year.

"Daddy, he's such a neat person and he does so much for so many people. I wish there was something I could do for him."

At that moment it dawned on Katie. The book. It was falling apart. Her father owned a print shop. "Daddy, do you think we could fix the book for the Winter Spirit and give it to him as a Christmas present?" Katie asked, her heart racing. "Oh please, Daddy. I'll help. I can run the old press and help with the collating and binding. I've done it before. Pulleeeease! It would be such a nice surprise."

Erik listened as Katie explained about the book and how much she thought it would mean to her new friend. When he put his hand to his chin, Katie stopped talking. She had known her dad long enough to know that this gesture meant he was weighing an idea in his head.

fter a few moments, he smiled. Mending the book would be a great deed for Hans and it would mean the world to Katie. Imagine, being able to help Santa Claus? "OK, Katie Bear. Let's see what we can do," Erik said.

Katie waited until the truck reached a red light. Then she took off her seat belt and gave her dad a great big hug. "I love you," she said. "It's going to be the best Christmas ever!"

The next day Erik told his employees what he and Katie hoped to do and everyone at the plant — even Uncle Junior, the grumpy old printer who only worked two days a week — seemed eager to help. While an editor and a graphic artist went to work on the inside pages, Katie and her dad picked out the leather for the book's cover. Katie looked the colors and textures over and over in her dad's office. Her dad had time to drink a cup of tea and finish a sandwich before Katie let out a holler.

"I found it! I found the perfect color of green!" She held up a swatch of leather. "And see! It even looks like it was brushed with evergreen needles."

"Great," Erik said. "I'll place a rush on the order today."

atie lived in a small town where news travels fast. When their neighbors and the teachers at the pre-school heard about the wonderful book and its contents many of them stopped by the shop to investigate. Even Katie's mum, Edwina, came to see how the project was coming along.

"Have you read this book?" Edwina asked Katie. "The artwork is incredible and the words ... I had to stop. I felt like I was reading someone's diary, the diary of St. Nick!"

Katie hugged her mother. "I know," she whispered in her ear. "The Winter Spirit told me it contains all of the stories that he has heard from people around the world. Do you think we should have Daddy put a title page on it? We could call it, 'Santa's Secrets!' or how about, 'The Diary of the Winter Spirit'?"

The graphic artists scanned all of the Winter Spirit's old drawings and doodles into the computer and enhanced the ones that were faded and difficult to see.

They looked as if he had just finished sketching them. All of the crispy white pages were bound together by a dark green leather cover with the initials, "WS" embossed on its front. At the back of the book Katie's dad added lined blank pages, so Hans could enter future stories, and a bigger pocket to hold the letters and loose notes he might collect over the years. Everyone agreed, it looked truly magical. Uncle Junior had a tear in his eye as Katie held it up in the shop so everyone could see the finished product.

On Christmas Eve, the newly bound book sat on a table in Katie's house, waiting for its owner to arrive. That day, Joanie, who had helped with the book along with her little brother, Cookie, paid Katie a visit. Cookie's real name was Conrad, but he loved Oreos and for obvious reasons was called "Cookie."

"I know we don't usually give each other presents, but this year I couldn't help it," Joanie said, handing Katie a package wrapped in purple paper.

Katie opened the gift. It was a pewter sculpture of Santa Claus with a note attached where Joanie had written, "I believe in the Winter Spirit too."

Katie hugged Joanie. She truly was her best friend.

Joanie and her brother took off for home, but as soon as the two of them reached the end of Katie's driveway, Joanie turned and yelled. "Hey, but it's our secret ok?"

Katie and her family attended church on Christmas Eve. Then they enjoyed a wonderful dinner at her grandparents' home. She didn't hear from the Winter Spirit but she wasn't surprised. She knew about his good work and that alone warmed her heart.

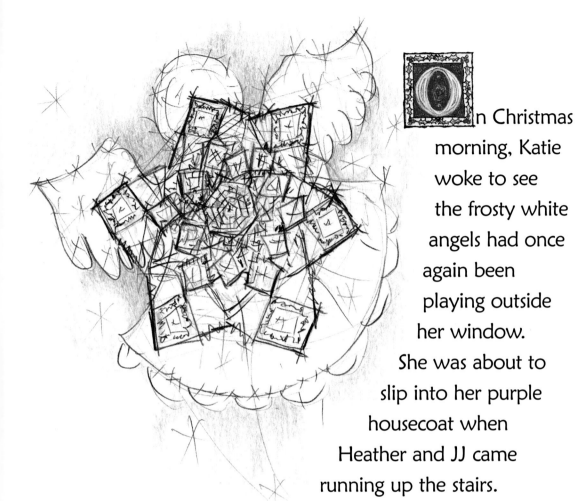

On Christmas morning, Katie woke to see the frosty white angels had once again been playing outside her window. She was about to slip into her purple housecoat when Heather and JJ came running up the stairs.

"Katie, Katie," they yelled. "Santa was here. Santa was here and he took his book. Come see! Come see what he left you by the tree!"

Katie's heart started to race and her head got dizzy. "Whatdaya mean he took the book?" she sputtered, while stumbling down the stairs.

Erik and Edwina were standing next to the tree waiting for Katie and her siblings.

Sitting on the hearth next to them was a hand-carved wooden Santa Claus. It had a big red bow tied at its waist. Katie stared at the figure. "It's the Winter Spirit," Katie said, recognizing the face and coat. "It looks just like him."

Erik handed Katie an ivory envelope sealed with a shiny red stamp embossed with the letters: WS. Erik told Katie that he found the note sitting on the mantel next to the figurine. It was addressed, "To Katie"

"Open it. Open it, Katie," JJ said.

"Yeah. Hurry up," said Heather.

Even Katie's parents were anxious for her to open it. Katie tore the red seal on the back and pulled out the sheet of parchment paper.

T he letter was written in cursive.

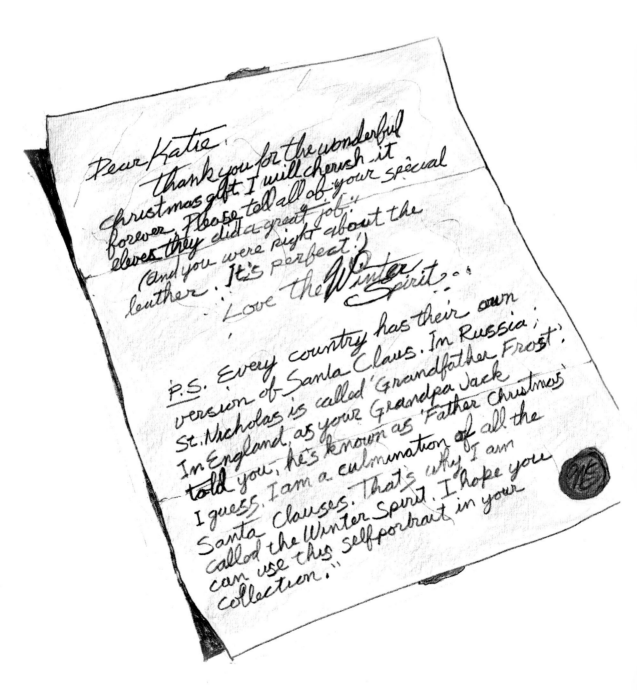

Dear Katie,

thank you for the wonderful christmas gift. I will cherish it forever. Please tell all of your special elves they did a great job.

(And you were right about the leather. It's perfect.)

Love the Winter Spirit...

P.S. Every country has their own version of Santa Claus. In Russia, St. Nicholas is called 'Grandfather Frost'. In England, as your Grandpa Jack told you, he's known as 'Father Christmas'. I guess, I am a culmination of all the Santa Clauses. That's why I am called the Winter Spirit. I hope you can use this selfportrait in your collection."

That night, Katie placed the Winter Spirit figurine on her dresser next to Father Christmas. Then she pulled out the shoebox from under her bed and added her letter from the Winter Spirit to the top of the pile. She was just about to close the lid on the box when she noticed something about the return address.

"Oh my goodness," Katie gasped, sitting back on her heels. "It's the same address. It's just like all of my other letters.

Santa Claus really does live on Reindeer Ranch Road!"

atie has never seen Hans again.

But every Christmas she receives a letter telling her about
the latest adventure of the Winter Spirit.

Another Story to tell...

Angels: The Spirited Messengers

A little girl asked me once, "Do you believe in angels?" I looked at the child, who appeared to be an angel herself. She had long curls that fell in ringlets over her shoulders and her eyes ... they sparkled like the ocean on a sunny day.

"Yes," I said. "Don't you?"

The little girl shrugged her shoulders.

"Have you ever been afraid of something?" I asked her. "Perhaps you were sleeping and you heard a noise that woke you up. When you opened your eyes it was dark and you got scared. Then suddenly, for some reason, you felt better and went back to sleep."

The little girl jumped up and down.

"Yes. Yes," she said.

"Well, that was your guardian angel," I said.

The word angel can mean "one going" or "one sent," as in a messenger. It is a common belief that angels are the spiritual liaisons between God and humans.

Looking to the heavens tonight, I am reminded of the angels who delivered a message to the shepherds living out in the fields, keeping watch over their flocks at night.

"And the angel said unto them. Fear not: for, behold, I bring you good tidings of great joy, which shall be to all people. For unto you is born this day in the city of David a Savior, which is Christ the Lord. And this shall be a sign unto you; Ye shall find the baby wrapped in swaddling clothes, lying in a manger. And suddenly there was with the angel a multitude of the heavenly host praising God, and saying, Glory to God in the highest, and on earth peace, good will toward men."

(Luke 2:10-12).

Boxing Day (Dec. 26)

On this day, I am usually very tired but in a happy, jubilant kind of way. In countries such as the Bahamas, Canada, Australia and England, Dec. 26 is known as Boxing Day. It's said to have originated, a long time ago when people were employed as servants to wealthy landowners. On Christmas Day, servants had to work. It was their duty to see to the needs of their employer and his or her family members. The day after Christmas the servants were presented with a box containing leftovers from the previous day's dinner, a special gift or a bonus, and the day off. Historically, the churches of England also would empty the alms boxes (boxes where people would place monetary donations) and give the money to the poor.

Today, most people don't have servants, but the day is still recognized as a holiday. For me, Boxing Day is the one day of the year when I'm sure my work is done.

Candy Canes: Medicinal Candy

What's a beautiful Christmas tree without a sweet collection of red and white candy canes? Just a nice evergreen. Some people believe that a shopkeeper created them as a special treat for his children. Others talk about a clumsy elf who tripped in the candy factory and spilled red sugar into a batch of white candy canes, thus creating the first striped candy cane.

To the best of my knowledge, candy canes have been around since the Middle Ages. Monks used to make a medicine for coughs and colds using a variety of ingredients including wintergreen and peppermint. No child likes to take medicine. But every child loves candy. So, the monks blended the ingredients for the medicine with sugar to create a sweet treat. It was molded into a stick with a curved end so it could be hung up to harden. The curved end resembles a shepherd's crook and when turned upside down, the letter J for Jesus. Jesus was considered to be the shepherd of his people. Having these two relationships was also good medicine.

Candles: A Light in the World

Many people believe that the warm glow of a candle keeps away evil spirits. I would have to agree. I always feel comforted by the light of a candle. When Jesus was born, he was said to be the Light of the World, which is why a candle is lit during many Christian celebrations. One of the most important parts of modern day Hanukkah celebrations is the lighting of candles: one the first night, one the second, and so on until all of the candles have been lit in a special candelabra called a menorah.

Carols: Singing Songs of Joy

In England long ago, there were groups of people known as mummers. Not mummies, mummers. Mummers were performers who would dress up in elaborate costumes and sing songs for people in the community. Sometimes they would perform for crowds gathered at the church, other times they would travel through the neighborhoods, visiting family and friends. The mummers were rewarded with food and drinks such as hot apple cider. If you happen to get a visit from a mummer on Christmas Eve be sure to invite them in. It is believed that a visit from a mummer on this special night means you will have good luck in the New Year.

As long as I can remember songs have been a part of the winter holiday season. In ancient times, songs were sung around large campfires to celebrate the winter solstice.

I love Christmas carols. 'Silent Night' reminds me of the wonderful evenings when I am riding in my sleigh, my vision guided by the light of the moon and my progress powered by a cool December breeze.

However, I wish someone would write a new Christmas song. I'd like that.

Christmas Bells: Instruments of Celebration

A long time ago in Bethlehem, the night's silence was broken by the sound of a crying baby and the ringing of bells hanging around the neck of the stable's sheep.

Bells have always been a part of celebrations, especially those surrounding Christmas and the winter solstice. I don't know if it's the cold December air or the winter winds, but I think the sweetest sounds come from a bell rung on Christmas Eve.

Christmas Trees: Forever Green

Since it was the only plant that stayed green all year round, ancient people believed evergreens were sacred. They called it the "Tree of Life."

When I visit today's homes I smell lemon lime and peach mango, but a long time ago a good potpourri was made of orange rinds and pine needles. During the winter, when homes were closed to shield residents from the cold, evergreen branches served as air fresheners, as stuffing for mattresses, and as beautiful decorations. The evergreen's pine sap was used by children as chewing gum.

Martin Luther was said to be the first person to light the Christmas tree. According to historians the idea came to him during a moonlight walk in the woods. A whistling amidst the pines overhead made him look to the sky. There, through the bows of the evergreen shone the brilliant stars of December. Wanting to share the majestic sight, Luther cut down a small evergreen tree and placed it in his home. He recreated the spectacle of stars using candles, which he placed on the evergreen's branches.

Find the Pickle in the Tree

One Christmas, I received a small box in addition to many wonderful cards and letters. In it was a bright green pickle. I could tell by the gold ring at the top and by its silver hook that it was meant to be a Christmas ornament. Upon closer look I found a note explaining its origin and meaning.

Legend has it that three young men went missing after stopping at a local pub in a small village. The young men were all very rich and had stopped at an Inn owned by two very bad people. St. Nicholas, who was visiting at the time, had dreamt about the missing young men. The dream led him to the Inn, where he found the young men packed in pickle barrels. St. Nicholas said a prayer for the young men, who were then saved. It is for this reason that St. Nicholas is known as the patron saint of young men. It's also the reason for the pickle ornament. Every Christmas, a pickle should be hidden among the branches of the evergreen tree and on Christmas morning the first person to find the pickle should receive a special gift and good luck the whole year through. Believe me, the pickle is harder to find then you think.

Hanging of Stockings

Thousands of children hang up their stockings on Christmas Eve hoping that St. Nicholas will fill them with an assortment of treasures. You never know what you will find. One year, the stocking could contain chocolates, nuts and fruit. Another year, it could be stuffed with gummy worms, a whistle or a flute. What makes the tradition so much fun is not what Santa Claus leaves inside but the fact that it's a surprise!

Yahooeee! As one little girl I know would say.

St. Nicholas was a very rich man, but charitable in the truest meaning of the word.

It's been said that it was after he helped a poor merchant that this Christmas tradition began. One of my favorite variations of this story has St. Nicholas coming to the aid of a widow from Myra.

The widow's husband had been a rich merchant but then he fell onto hard times and when he died, he left her and their three daughters penniless. The widow worked hard to keep the business that had been in her husband's family for so many years, but without success. Eventually she and the girls had to take in laundry in exchange for food.

When St. Nicholas heard that the merchant's wife and daughters were starving, he decided to help. Wanting to remain anonymous, St. Nicholas waited until dark and crept to the family's little seaside cottage. He tossed three bags of gold through an open window.

It just so happened that it was one of the nights when the women had washed a huge load of socks in order to get a little bread and milk for supper. All of the stockings from the wash were hung by the fire to dry. When St. Nicholas threw the coins through the window that's where they landed. Plop! Into the stockings.

The next morning when the sisters woke up they found the socks full of gold They cried tears of joy and on that Christmas Day, for the first time in many weeks, the woman and her three daughters ate until their stomachs were full and then slept comfortably in their beds. The widow was able to buy back the family store and pay for the dowry of her three girls, who lived happily ever after.

Of course, the widow shared her news with everyone she knew and the following year every mantel in town was adorned with clean washed stockings.

When children ask me why Santa Claus is so secretive I share this story with them because it illustrates that good deeds should never be done for recognition, but out of pure kindness.

Hanukkah

About the time of the winter solstice comes Hanukkah, a religious holiday celebrated by Jewish people. A long time ago, the ruler Antiochus forbid the people of Israel to practice their religion. After several years of oppression, the Jews revolted and reclaimed the Holy Temple of Jerusalem and their right to religious freedom.

After the victory, the people cleaned the temple and polished the menorah but upon starting the rededication service, according to tradition, only a one-day supply of sacred oil could be found. To their surprise the small quantity of oil burned miraculously for eight days. Today, Jewish families and their friends gather to help light the candles in the menorah in commemoration of that miracle and their ancestor's fight for religious freedom. It is a time of generosity and remembrance, holiday fun, good food and joyous family gatherings.

Holly

It's a plant similar to the evergreen but it bears red fruit in the winter. Romans used it for decorations during the Saturnalia Festival. Traditionally a ring of holly was used to depict the ring of thorns that Jesus wore during his walk to the cross. The red berries represent the blood of Jesus.

Kwanzaa (Dec. 26)

Kwanzaa is not a religious holiday. It is a celebration recognizing the goodness of families, friends and the community. Kwanzaa, meaning "First Fruits", was created by Dr. Maulana Karenga in 1966, in an effort to promote, revitalize and preserve African-American culture. It is based on seven principles: Umoja (unity), Kujichagulia (self-determination), Ujima (collective work and responsibility), Ujamaa (cooperative economics), Nia (purpose), Kuumba (creativity) and Imani (faith). The 7-day holiday is celebrated from Dec. 26 through Jan. 1 by millions of people in the United States and around the world.

Mistletoe

A long time ago, people used this tiny plant for medicinal purposes. Since it enabled them to cure so many ailments, it was considered magical, even sacred. Some people believed the area surrounding the plant was also sacred. This understood, it was not uncommon to see a warrior who happened upon such a place throw down his weapon and extend his hand in peace.

Today, mistletoe is hung in archways and entrances. During the holiday season it marks the spot where all differences are to be left behind. Those who pass under it are given an okay from cupid to steal a kiss.

Ornaments: The Fruits of the Christmas Tree

Decorating trees with ornaments is an old tradition that dates back to the Romans and the celebration of Saturnalia. During the holiday fruits and nuts were placed on the tree as offerings to the gods. The people wanted to make sure that the tree would remain green during the winter season. Today's ornaments are made out of all sorts of materials but a long time ago they were made primarily out of wood. When glass was developed the ornaments were blown into shapes, like pickles.

Poinsettias

A story was told that when
Mary and Joseph were fleeing
to Egypt to escape the wrath
of Herod, baby Jesus knew
what was happening. During
their escape, Jesus spotted an
unimpressive weed growing by
the roadside. He touched the plant
and immediately its leaves turned red. Today, it remains
red as a reminder of the innocent children who died under
Herod's rule.

Reindeer

The ancient god Odin from Scandinavian mythology
used flying reindeer to pull the sled he used to deliver gifts
to his subjects. In Finland, reindeer are
plentiful and are used like horses to pull
wagons, carts, and sleighs. A little boy
scoffed at the reindeer on my staff.
"Reindeers can't fly," he said. I looked
him in the eyes and asked, "Have you
ever seen a reindeer scurry across a
snowy mountainside? If you have, then
you know as soon as they hit the edge of the
mountain, they do fly, up and away."

Reindeer flight food: Mix one pail of chopped oats with water, then add one teaspoon of levitation formula per hour of flight.

Santa Claus, aka...

The world is a sleigh filled with many wonderful people, cultures and languages. "Gezuar Krishlindjet!" is Albanian for Merry Christmas and "Godt Nytar!" is Danish for Happy New Year. There are hundreds of ways to greet a friend or family member during the holiday season. Is it any wonder then that there are also so many ways to say Santa Claus? Here's my list so far: Babbo Natale, Bacchus, Razi, Criscringle, Christkind, Christkindl, Christkindlein, Christndl, Ded Moroz, Father Christmas, Father Frost, Grandfather Frost, Grandfather Winter, Green Knight, Green Man, Hagios Nikolaos, Joulluppullo, Joulupukki, Julenisse, Julenissen, Kerstman, Kris Kringle, Nick, Noel Babba, Odin-Woden, Old St. Nick, Pa Norsk, Papa Noel, Pierre Noel, Pere Noel, Sabdiklos, Sancte Claus, Saint Nicholas, Santa Claus, Santa No Ojisan, Shengdan Laoren, Sinter Klass, St. Basil, The Gift Giver, The Old Man of Winter, Uncle Santa, Weinachtsmann, The Winter Spirit and St. Lucia.

St. Lucia, the only girl among all these Winter Spirits, is known as the patron saint of the blind and is the gift giver Scandinavia. Legend has it, when Christians were hiding in underground tunnels for fear of being persecuted for their faith, Lucia, wearing a candlelit wreath on her head in order to see in the dark tunnels, brought food to the weary Christians.

Santa Claus Cookies: Sweet Gestures

What is it that makes a chocolate chip cookie taste so good? Is it the sugar or the sweet chocolate morsels? Neither. When a plate of cookies and a cold glass of milk are left for me I see it as an act of kindness and a sweet gesture of thanks. That is what makes them so good. Cookies also provide Santa Claus with nourishment for his long and arduous journey. I love cookies but one time I was offered a plate of smoked oysters and saltine crackers. It was a nice change.

A few years ago I received a beautiful Christmas letter from an Italian woman thanking me for a gift that I brought to her grandson, Michael. Along with the letter was a package of sugar cookies. They were wonderful, not too sweet and not too dry. Taped to the cookie tin's lid was a recipe. The woman said that she had inherited it from her mother, who lives in Italy.

Mama Borghi's sugar cookies

2 1/4 cups of sifted flour
1 1/2 tsp. baking powder
1 cup sugar
1/2 tsp. nutmeg
1/2 cup butter
2 eggs well beaten
1 tbsp milk

Mix the flour with the baking powder and nutmeg. In a separate bowl cream the butter thoroughly. Add sugar gradually until light and fluffy. Then fold in eggs and milk and beat well. Add small amounts of the flour mixture and beat after each addition until smooth. Roll the cookie mixture out on a slightly floured cutting board. Using holiday cookie cutters cut out fancy shapes.

Bake in oven at 425° Fahrenheit for seven minutes. It should make 2 1/2 dozen cookies.

Decorate with red, white and green sugar or colorful frosting.

Santa's Helpers

Santa's global network: Every year, a multitude of people around the world, do what they can to bring the spirit of Christmas to the poor, sick, elderly and unnoticed. There are the bell ringers who stand on wind-swept sidewalks singing Christmas carols and wishing shoppers a 'Merry Christmas' or 'Happy Holiday!' And there are also the guys and gals who work with charitable organizations, church groups and the community to help out families in need. How many grandfathers have told the story about the day the church pastor came to their house? How wonderful it was to receive a box filled with Christmas tangibles like new shoes and underwear, and gifts like a doll and a book? There are the military volunteers who track Santa Claus' journey on Christmas Eve and answer the calls of soldiers overseas. And many who make individual sacrifices, like the pediatric nurse who stays after her shift to nurture a premature infant who won't be going home on Christmas day. There are teachers who motivate their students to think about children less fortunate than themselves, and corporate sponsors who stock the city's food pantry shelves. There are the moms who bake cookies and cakes for Christmas bake sales and the dads who use their trucks and vans to deliver toys to the tots. Everywhere around the world Santa Claus has helpers who do what they can to bring the spirit of Christmas to those in need. I appreciate them all.

Santa's Sleigh

Santa's sleigh is just one of many vehicles that he has used to deliver gifts. In Holland, he is said to ride a white horse. In other parts of the world, he has been seen riding a cart hauled by a goat or donkey. Washington Irving wrote that St. Nicholas rode a wagon pulled by a horse that flew along the tops of trees. In the land of snow, nothing beats a sleigh pulled by eight reindeer. Ho, ho, ho. I'll never forget that little boy who said he saw me riding in a green SUV.

The boy was right. I loved that truck. It had an adapter for a cup warmer. I had the hot chocolate going all night.

Saturnalia : A Roman Holiday

One of the oldest festivals celebrated by Romans was that of the Saturnalia festival. It was a winter celebration that included feasting, dancing, singing, and gift giving. It was held in honor of the gods Saturn and Jupiter. During the festival, Romans would decorate evergreens with fruits and nuts. Legend has it that when Jupiter defeated Saturn to become the head god, he used a holly branch. This is one of the reasons why holly is associated with December celebrations.

Also during this time, Bachus, who is the god of wine, led a festival that celebrated the season's harvest of new wine.

Snowmen

Throughout the centuries, people have carved images out of the materials they had at hand. Mountain people were known to make tools and weapons out of stone. In areas where straw was readily available people would bundle the straw together and create statues. In parts of the world where the climate is cold, snow is the material people use to carve animals, houses and forts. I know of one man who made a large snow bear for his son. Over the years, many songs and stories have been written about snowmen and the magic they seem to have.

When I am traveling at night nothing makes me feel better than to see the horizon dotted with snow people. It's a sign that children are having fun.

Winter Solstice

North of the equator, the day with the fewest hours of light and the longest time of darkness usually falls between December 20 and 23. When it passes, the days get longer. This we know.

However, a long time ago people worried about the shortening of day. As winter grew closer and the nights grew longer they believed the earth was dying and that the sun would never come back. For when they saw that after Dec. 21 the sun's time over the earth grew longer and longer again, they celebrated its return. Traditionally, people would gather outside around a bonfire and sing winter songs. Solstice means a stoppage of the sun, which is why the celebration is known as the winter solstice.

A Young Bishop Named Nicholas

St. Nicholas lived a long time ago in a town along the Agean Sea. Orphaned at a young age, St. Nicholas was raised by monks in a monastery. St. Nicholas' parents were very rich and he inherited a sizeable amount of money. While he enjoyed using his inheritance to help the poor, his greatest joy was derived from helping children. He delighted in giving them gifts. Sometimes it would be a toy or a new pair of shoes, other times a pretty silver cup. St. Nicholas always seemed to know their hearts' desire.

Throughout his life, St. Nicholas was known to travel by sea to faraway lands. During one of his voyages, deadly storms threatened the lives of St. Nicholas and the ship's crew. St. Nicholas, believing strongly in the power of prayer, knelt and asked God to deliver his friends to safety. The seas calmed. During another storm, a sailor fell from the crow's nest to the deck. St. Nicholas knelt over the lifeless body and prayed. The sailor woke up. For this reason St. Nick is known as the patron saint of seafarers.

Another time St. Nicholas persuaded a couple thieves to return their looted goods and this is why he is also known as the patron saint of thieves. For other reasons, he is known as the patron saint of: pawn brokers, prisoners, young maidens, bankers, children young men, perfumers, bakers, shopkeepers, and wolves.

His remains are entombed in Italy. It's been reported that every year, a vile of liquid, with great curative powers, is extracted from his tomb. St. Nicholas' name day is December 6, which also happens to be Katie's birthday.

Winter Spirit: A Perfect Night

There once was a man who likened himself to me. Ever since he was a little boy, Santa Claus would make a special appearance at his house on Christmas Eve. He recalled waiting patiently by the tree for the annual visit, listening intently for the bells and the knock on the door. As he grew up, he realized, with some sadness, that the visiting Santa Claus was either his father, brother, or even sister. Still, he enjoyed the thrill of seeing the person in the bright red suit carrying a sack of toys over the stoop. The tradition continued until, one day, it was his turn to wear the suit. He enjoyed the task so much, he extended his visits to other families he knew.

One year, just before Christmas, a terrible accident rocked the neighborhood. A school bus stalled on a railway crossing and was hit by a train. No child was killed, but many were seriously injured.

On Christmas Eve, the young man donned his red suit and headed out the door. It was a postcard evening. The sky was navy blue and the lights on the trees and houses sparkled against the new fallen snow. He was headed to his sister's house, but was lured to a home with a magnificent display of white and red lights. The residents of the home were delighted by his visit. As he left the house, a man came running after him. He asked the young man if he would visit his neighbor's child, a little boy who had been injured in the school bus accident. The man said that the boy's parents were very distraught. They had promised their son, who was in the hospital and worried that Santa Claus wouldn't know where he was, that they would make sure Santa Claus paid him a visit. The parents had figured that they would hire an actor, but as it turned out, none had been available.

The young man went to the boy's house, knocked on the door and rang the bells on his belt, just as his father had done when he was a boy. A lovely woman opened the door. Her jaw dropped, and her eyes filled with tears.

"This is amazing," she said "our prayers have been answered." The mother then explained that she and the father had been just about to walk out the door on their way to the hospital and of course they had been so sad that they couldn't bring their son Santa Claus, as he had wished.

The little boy was pleased to see Santa Claus. He shook his hand and thanked him for the candy cane. Then, he turned to his parents and with love in his eyes wished them a Merry Christmas. They were the heroes in his eyes. They had brought him Santa Claus.

To this day, the young man, now older and wiser talks about the night he discovered the spirit of Santa Claus. Everything had fallen into place so perfectly. It was clear to him that something magical had intervened. How else could he have known the exact moment to stop by the house? A few minutes later and he would have missed the parent's departure.

It had been a perfect night.